nickelodeon.
Dora & Diego

DORA AND DIEGO HELP THE DINOSAUR

adapted by Lara Bergen and Ellie Seiss
based on the screenplay "Diego's Great Dinosaur Rescue"
written by Valerie Walsh
illustrated by Art Mawhinney

Ready-to-Read

Simon Spotlight/Nickelodeon
New York   London   Toronto   Sydney

Portions of this work were previously published in *Diego and the Dinosaurs* and *Diego's Great Dinosaur Rescue*.

Based on the TV series *Dora the Explorer*™ and *Go, Diego, Go!*™ as seen on Nick Jr.™

SIMON SPOTLIGHT/NICKELODEON
An imprint of Simon & Schuster Children's Publishing Division
1230 Avenue of the Americas, New York, New York 10020
For information about special discounts for bulk purchases, please contact
Simon & Schuster Special Sales at 1-866-506-1949 or
business@simonandschuster.com.
Manufactured in the United States of America 1210 LAK
This Simon Spotlight edition 2011
2 4 6 8 10 9 7 5 3 1
ISBN 978-1-4424-1400-6

Portions of this work were previously published in
Diego and the Dinosaurs and *Diego's Great Dinosaur Rescue.*

Hi, I am DIEGO,

and this is my cousin ! DORA

Today we are learning

all about . DINOSAURS

Do you like ? DINOSAURS

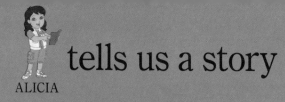 tells us a story
ALICIA

about a dinosaur named .
MAIA

The washed away
RAIN

her family's .
FOOTPRINTS

Now 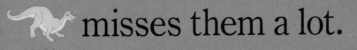 cannot
MAIA

find her family.

 misses them a lot.
MAIA

We have to help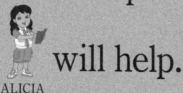
MAIA

find her family.

I will help.

 will help.
ALICIA

 will help.

DORA

 will help.

BABY JAGUAR

Will you help?

Great!

We need to jump back
to the time of the  DINOSAURS.
Jump! Jump! Jump!

Here we are

in the time of the .
DINOSAURS

Do you see a dinosaur ?
FOOTPRINT

Me too!

I think it is 's .
MAIA   FOOTPRINT

Let's follow it!

Look! There is .
MAIA

She is looking for her family.

Let's help her!

I know!

I will use my SPOTTING SCOPE

to find MAIA's family.

Do you see  's family

MAIA

in my ?

SPOTTING SCOPE

Yes! There they are.

They are on !

EGG ISLAND

We are on our way!

But wait!

 is hungry.
MAIA

She is a plant eater.

She eats .
LEAVES

Do you see a  TREE

with lots of LEAVES?

Yum!

Now we have to cross

the Rocky  cliffs.
ROCK

But look out!

There is a  slide!
ROCK

We need something soft
to land on.

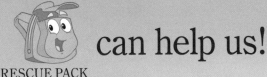

RESCUE PACK can help us!

 here!

RESCUE PACK

Are  soft to land on?

ROLLER SKATES

No!

Is a soft to land on?

TENNIS RACKET

No!

Is a big soft to land on?

PILLOW

Yes!

Thanks,  !

RESCUE PACK

How will we get back

to the top of the cliff?

ROCK

We can climb up

's long !

MAIA   TAIL

Thanks, !

MAIA

Look! There is ⬜ 🏔 !
EGG ISLAND

But how will we get

across the 🌊 ?
WATER

Did you know that lots of
could swim?

DINOSAURS

 can swim across the .

MAIA WATER

She can carry us on her back.

Hooray! We made it to
EGG ISLAND

And look!

There is 's family!
MAIA

Do you see their
NEST

full of ? 🥚
EGGS

We did it!

We helped  get home.

MAIA

Thank you for helping!